MW01615147

Contents

T Can't Stop Reading

The nail place was a little stinky, but T didn't mind. Mama Rex had bought him a new book.

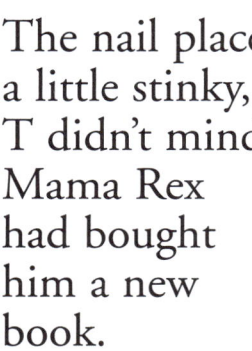

It was a funny book. T laughed so hard he fell right over.

Mama Rex and T

"I love reading," yelled T. "I wish I could read everything in the entire world!"

So T sat back down to do it. He hasn't finished yet.

3

Story by Rachel Vail
Illustrations by Steve Björkman

Kids on Mars Read All Day

Horus reads his cereal box at breakfast.

Pelly reads poems to her pet slog.

First Graders from Mars

Tera reads the teacher's words on the board.

And every night Nergal reads his favorite book to his mom.

5

Story by Shana Corey
Illustrations by Mark Teague

"Trick or Read!"

It was October 31st and all the children were dressed up for Halloween.

"You look like The Mummy," Felicia said
6   to Peter. "Want to guess who I am?"

"That's easy," said Peter. "You're the Statue of Liberty."

"Close," said Felicia. "I'm the Statue of Libraries!"

7

Story and Illustrations by
Peter Maloney and Felicia Zekauskas

Heroes Love to Read

Ricky Ricotta and his Mighty Robot love to beat the bad guys, but they always find the best adventures in books!

Ricky Ricotta's Mighty Robot

Story by Dav Pilkey

Illustration by Martin Ontiveros